Chesapeake
RAINBOW

by Priscilla Cummings
illustrated by David Aiken

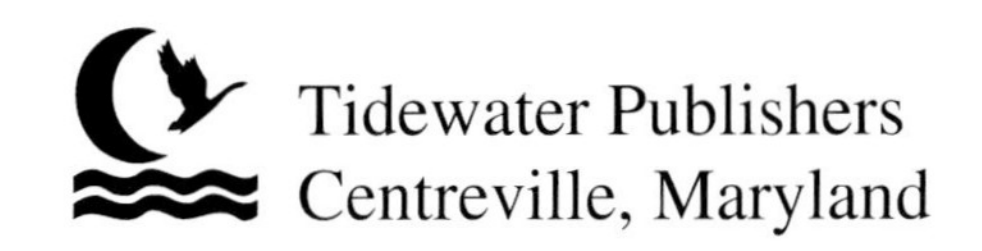

How many colors
Has the Chesapeake Bay?
More than a rainbow,
You could say.

Blue is the color of the water in the Bay,
And blue is the color of a perfect day.
The heron that we call Great Blue is blue.
The stripe down a crab's leg? It's blue, too.
Blue is a color of the Chesapeake Bay.
Let's think of another that we see everyday.

White is the color of the sail on a boat,
Of feathers on a swan, and a crabber's float.
A wave wears a cap of white foam when it swells,
And white is the color of oyster shells.
White is a color of the Chesapeake Bay.
Let's think of another that we see everyday.

Green is the color of cordgrass in the sand,
Of tall leafy cornstalks that grow on the land.
You see a green frog when the water's clean.
And square channel markers are always green.
Green is a color of the Chesapeake Bay.
Let's think of another that we see everyday.

3

Red is the color of the steamed crabs we eat,
Of ladybugs and strawberries—and sunburned feet!
Red cardinals and autumn leaves are fun to see.
And red channel markers are spotted easily.
Red is a color of the Chesapeake Bay.
Let's think of another that we see everyday.

2

Gray is the color of the morning fog,
Of squirrels and a fox and a very old log.
Some gray Navy ships cruise the Chesapeake,
And smooth, gray stones line the bottom of a creek.
Gray is a color of the Chesapeake Bay.
Let's think of another that we see everyday.

Yellow is the color of spring daffodils,
Of black-eyed Susans and many birds' bills.
A waterman's overalls are often yellow.
A gosling is, too, when he's a wee fellow.
Yellow is a color of the Chesapeake Bay.
Let's think of another that we see everyday.

Orange is the color of a sunset sky,
A tiger lily and a Monarch butterfly.
A baseball team wears some orange at the game.
The Orioles are named for a bird with that name!
Orange is a color of the Chesapeake Bay.
Let's think of another that we see everyday.

orioles
BALTIMORE

Black is the color of a midnight sky,
Of mussel shells, black bears, and buzzards up high.
Black is the color of an oyster shucker's glove,
And plump blackberries baked in pies we love.
Black is a color of the Chesapeake Bay.
Let's think of another that we see everyday.

Pink is a color of the dogwood trees
And rose vines bending low in the breeze.
The legs on some gulls are short and pink.
You see a pink tongue when a deer takes a drink.
Pink is a color of the Chesapeake Bay.
Let's think of another that we see everyday.

3

Brown is the color of a newborn fawn.
And branches of a tree with all its leaves gone.
Pelicans and mother ducks are shades of brown,
And brown is the color of the piers in town!
Brown is a color of the Chesapeake Bay.
Let's think of another that we see everyday.

Purple is the color of wisteria flowers
And thunderstorm clouds before the rain showers.
Purple-colored worms are often used for bait,
And tall purple irises grow by the gate.
Purple is a color of the Chesapeake Bay.
We've found quite a few, wouldn't you say?

How many colors
Has the Chesapeake Bay?
More than a rainbow
Everyday!